FARMER JOE
and the Music Show

P1-3

To Alice Blacker, The Old Crow Medicine Show
and The Hot Bang – T.M.

For Dylan,
with special thanks to Liz Johnson and Tim Rose,
for their wit and wisdom – G.P-R.

ORCHARD BOOKS
338 Euston Road, London NW1 3BH
Orchard Books Australia
Level 17/207 Kent Street, Sydney, NSW 2000

ISBN 978 1 40830 530 0

First published in 2008 by Orchard Books
First published in paperback in 2009

Text © Tony Mitton 2008
Illustrations © Guy Parker-Rees 2008

The rights of Tony Mitton to be identified
as the author and of Guy Parker-Rees to be
identified as the illustrator of this work have
been asserted by them in accordance with the
Copyrights, Designs and Patents Act, 1988.

A CIP catalogue record for this book is available
from the British Library.

1 3 5 7 9 10 8 6 4 2

Printed in China

Orchard Books is a division of Hachette Children's Books,
an Hachette Livre UK company.

www. hachettelivre.co.uk

FARMER JOE
and the Music Show

lyrics by
Tony Mitton

illustrations by
Guy Parker-Rees

ORCHARD BOOKS

Down on the farm of poor old Joe,
the hens won't lay and the crops won't grow.

The cows won't graze and the pigs won't feed,
and Joe just can't think what they need.

He puts on his hat and yells, **"Yee-har!"**

Then he starts to pluck on his old guitar.

Along the trail comes frisky Fox.

He pulls out a fiddle from a battered old box.

He tunes the strings

and he lifts the bow . . .

Out of a burrow pop two big ears.
Rabbit just loves
that stuff she hears.

She hops from her hole and starts to play
on a concertina, right away!

Concertina, wheee-hee-hah,
skiddly fiddle and old guitar.
The crops like the music. Me-oh-my!
Look at them stretching up to the sky!

Now, what's that rumbling, grumbling sound?
Something **big** is stumbling round.

Soon we'll see it face to face . . .

Wow! It's Bear with a double bass!
Doom-doom-doo

and **whoom- whoom- whum,**

Bear's bass booms with a deep, low thrum.

Joe's on guitar with Fox on the fiddle,
Rabbit's concertina fits in the middle,

the bees go buzz as they hum around
and Bear's bass booms as he stomps the ground.

Bull wakes up. What's this he hears?
"**Herd!**" he bellows.
"Now, lift your ears!"

The cows start mooing as the music plays,
then they click their hooves as they bend to graze.

The creatures caper — look at them go —
to the thrill of the hillbilly music show.

They **jump** and **jive.**
They **leap** and **bound.**
They love the rhythm of the country sound.

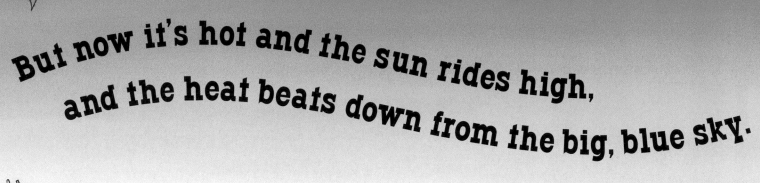

But now it's hot and the sun rides high,
and the heat beats down from the big, blue sky.

What'll they do now?
What do you think?
Sprawl in the shade with a nice, cool drink.

And Farmer Joe can smile and strum, and say, "Just let those sweet tunes come.

He thanks his friends
for the good they've done.
Then they play some more now,
just for fun.